This Manuscript Belongs To

Sir/Lady

_____

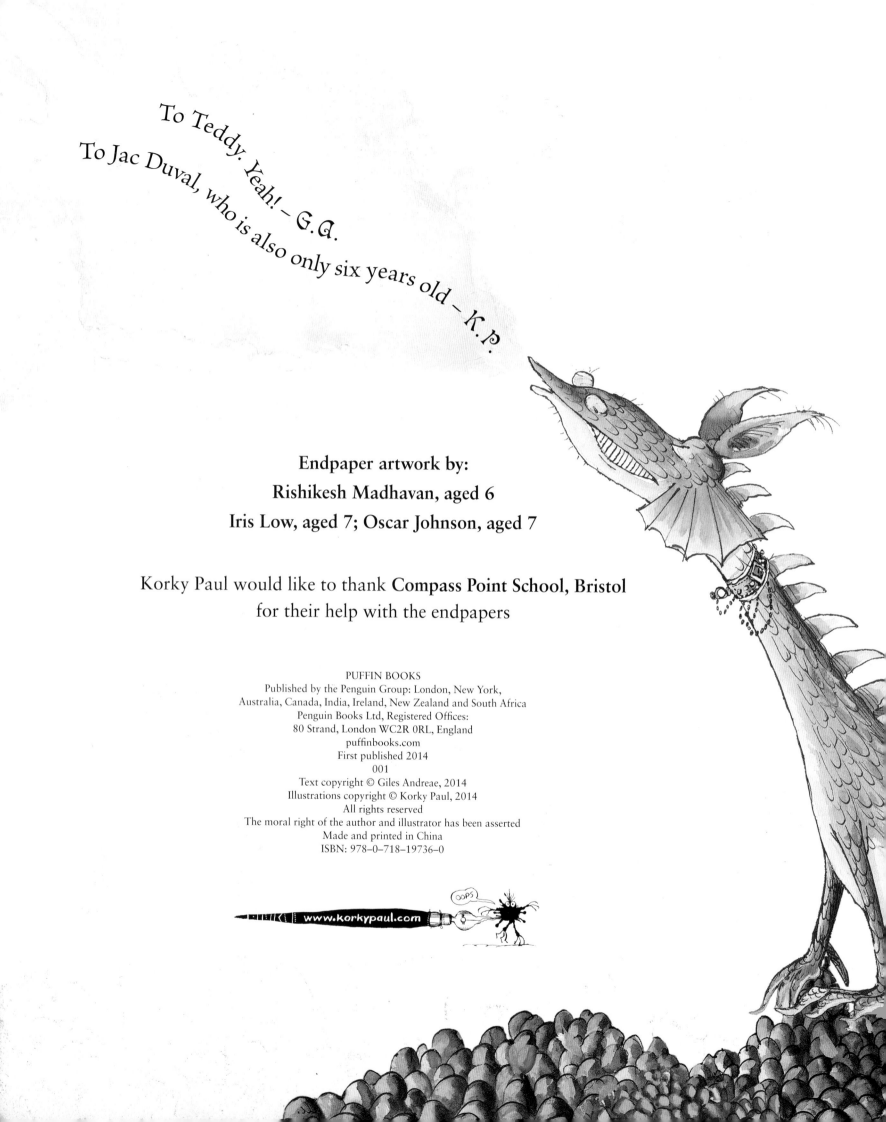

To Teddy. Yeah! – G.A.

To Jac Duval, who is also only six years old – K.P.

Endpaper artwork by:

Rishikesh Madhavan, aged 6

Iris Low, aged 7; Oscar Johnson, aged 7

Korky Paul would like to thank **Compass Point School, Bristol**
for their help with the endpapers

PUFFIN BOOKS
Published by the Penguin Group: London, New York,
Australia, Canada, India, Ireland, New Zealand and South Africa
Penguin Books Ltd, Registered Offices:
80 Strand, London WC2R 0RL, England
puffinbooks.com
First published 2014
001
Text copyright © Giles Andreae, 2014
Illustrations copyright © Korky Paul, 2014
All rights reserved
The moral right of the author and illustrator has been asserted
Made and printed in China
ISBN: 978–0–718–19736–0

www.korkypaul.com

OOPS

Sir Scallywag
~and the Deadly Dragon Poo

GILES ANDREAE

and KORKY PAUL

PUFFIN

There lived a king in ancient times
Who wasn't very brave.
He didn't look for knights to joust
Or damsels he could save . . .

And instead of fighting battles
And performing daring feats
King Colin simply lay in bed . . .
And guzzled loads of sweets.

He couldn't get enough of them
And neither could his queen,
So they spent their kingdom's fortune
On a giant sweet machine.

The king, the queen and all their
Knights grew lazy and grew fat.
Well, all except Sir Scallywag . . .
We'll soon come on to that.

For in a castle dark and cold
A rumour reached the ear
Of the fearsome Baron Greedyguts.
"What's this," he said, "I hear?

"A great BIG giant sweet machine?
Oh, what a prize to own!
I'm going to have to capture it
And bring it to MY home!

"I'll hatch a really EVIL plan . . .
Yes, this is what I'll do –
I'll bomb King Colin's castle
With some . . . stinky dragon poo!"

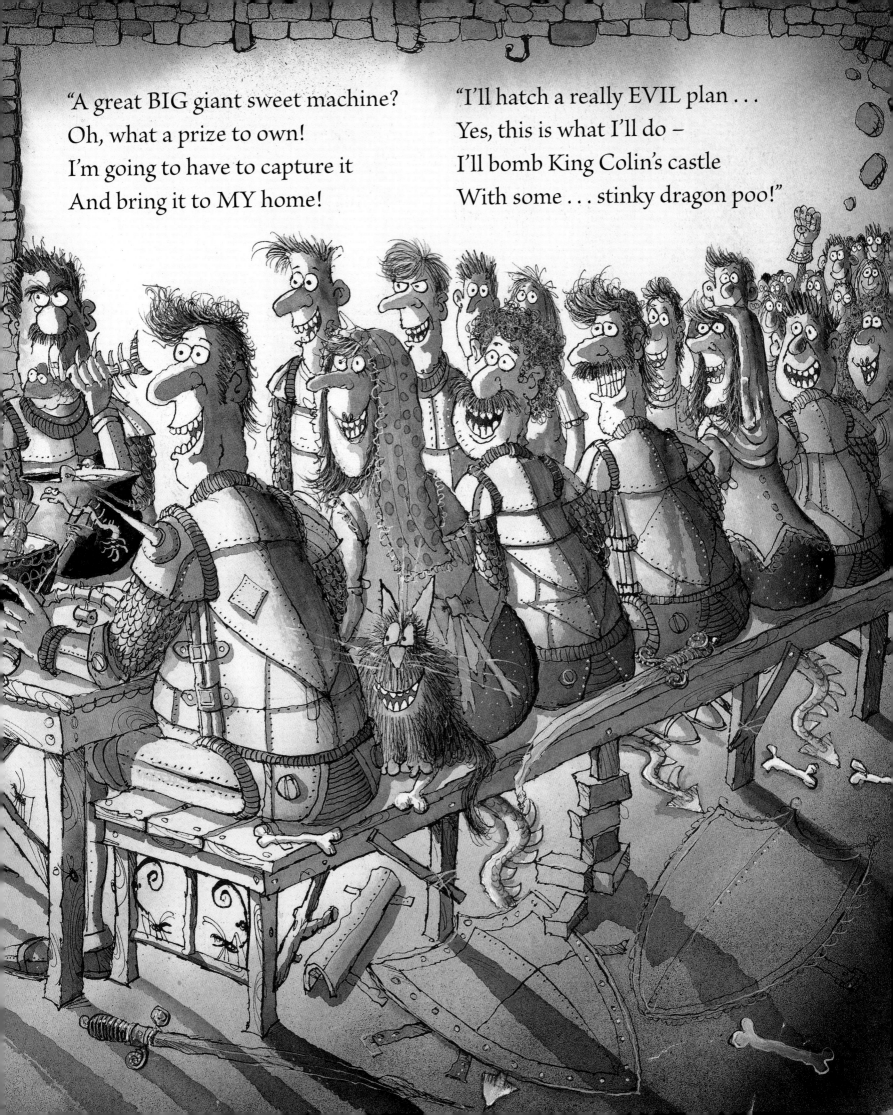

As it happened, Baron Greedyguts
Kept dragons as his pets.
He fed them rotten cabbages
And guess what happened next?

A rumbling and a grumbling sound
Began inside their tums
And soon the foulest dragon poo
Came gurgling from their bums.

"Quick, fetch the giant catapults!"
The Baron cried with glee,
"I'm starving, don't you know,
And I want sweeties for my tea!"

So, soon a great bombardment
Of King Colin had begun.
And all his useless knights could do
Was turn their backs and run.

"Oh, crikey!" cried King Colin.
"Yikes! I don't know what to do!
My castle's disappearing
Under piles of dragon poo!

"There's only one of all my knights
Who might just save the day.
Oh, help us, brave Sir Scallywag!
Oh, help us, please, I pray!"

The six-year-old Sir Scallywag
Appeared with sword in hand.
"I'm here for you, O King," he said,
"Your wish is my command."

"Oh, Scallywag!" King Colin cried.
"Whatever can be done?
Why is that meany, Greedyguts,
Bombarding us . . . with DUNG?!"

"I'll go and find out what I can,"
Said Scallywag. "You'll see . . .
I'm always up for challenges
So, please, leave this with me!"

He beckoned to his trusty steed:
"Come Roofus, through the gates!
We're going to spy on Greedyguts
And find out what awaits."

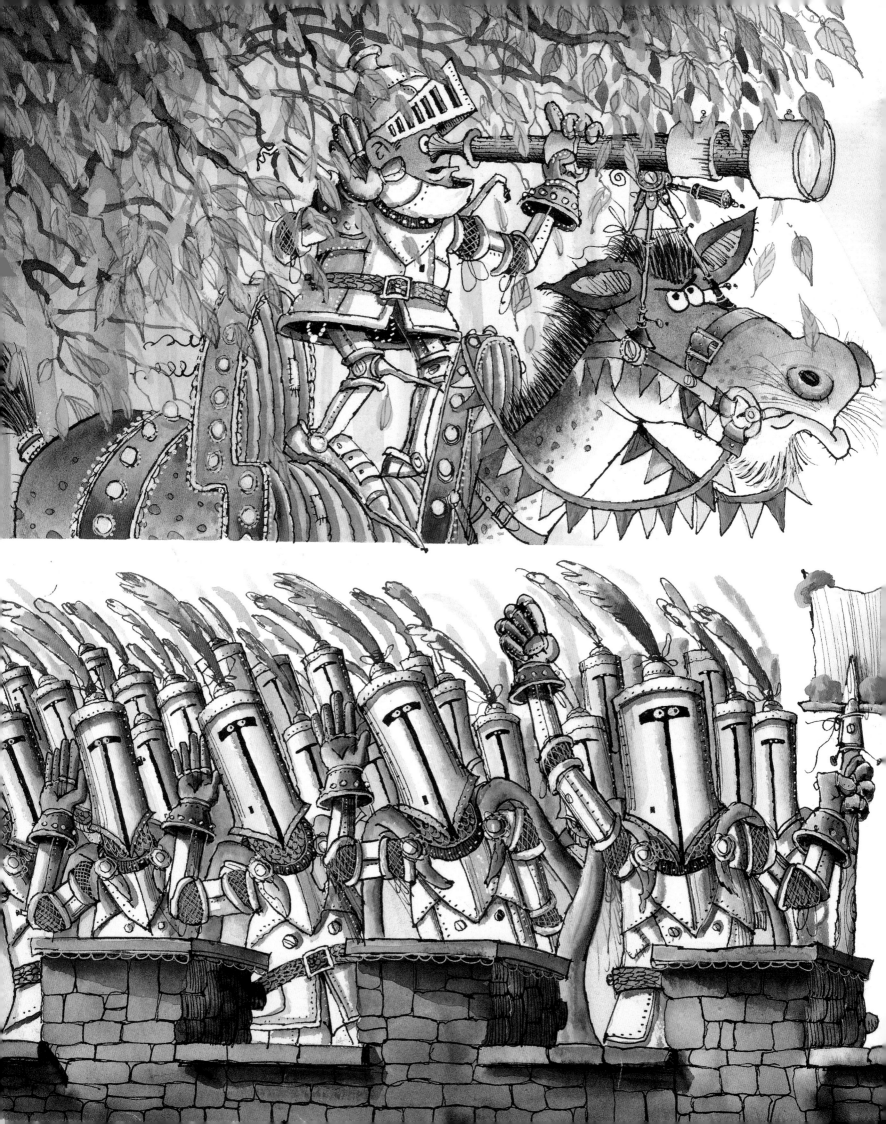

Old Greedyguts was pacing
Up and down his castle wall.
"This dragon poo's so stinky
That they'll have no strength at all!

"They'll be gagging! They'll be choking!
No, they'll never want to fight.
So let's invade King Colin's castle . . .

Let's invade tonight!"

Sir Scallywag came charging back
And told the king this news.
"But I've got a cunning plan," he said.
"Quick, scoop up all those poos!

"Let everyone get buckets.
Come on, fast as you can be . . .
Then fill them up to bursting
And deliver them to me!"

The knights all did as they were told –
He wouldn't let them stop
Until they'd made a mountain
Out of squelchy dragon plop.

Sir Scallywag then stuck his sword
In Colin's sweet machine.
He waggled it around
Until the thing began to steam.

It whistled, whirred and juddered,
Then he gave it a great kick.
"I think that's it," said Scallywag.
"Yes, that should do the trick!

"Now, all we have to do, my friends,
Is just sit back and wait.
I know it won't be long
Before the baron's at our gate."

And, sure enough, as night-time fell
King Colin heard the sound
Of a hundred knights in armour
Thundering across the ground.

"Now, steady," whispered Scallywag,
"Wait till you see their eyes.
That Greedyguts and all his knights
Are in for a surprise!"

"Attack them!" bellowed Greedyguts.
"Let no one here go free.
Now, where's that famous sweet machine?
It's coming home with me!"

"It's here," replied Sir Scallywag,
"If this is what you mean.
But I've changed it from a sweetie . . .

... to a giant poo machine!"

With that, he pulled a lever
And the thing began to hum.
Then, from the spout, there shot
A giant jet of dragon dung.

It hit the startled Greedyguts
Right in his pudgy face.
And soon a sea of dragon poo
Was surging through the place.

"Take that, you stinky poo-for-brains!"
Sir Scallywag then said
As he aimed another splurge of dung
At Greedyguts's head.

Sir Scallywag kept firing
Until all the knights were gone.
They were blasted from the kingdom
By the gloopy, sludgy pong.

"You've saved us!" cried King Colin.
"Oh, Sir Scallywag, hoorah!
Is there something we can do
To show how grateful we all are?"

"Well, since you've asked," said Scallywag,
"There is one little chore.
Command those lazy knights
To tidy up this castle floor!

"And, while they're at it, could you please
Go fetch some nails and wood.
Just one last change to this machine
Would do you all some good."

He sawed and screwed and hammered.
"Look, I'll fix this in a trice –
Ta-da! A brand-new, shiny, five-star . . .

"... exercise device!

"Now, on you get, you lazy oafs
Start pedalling ... FULL SPEED!
An army that is fighting fit
Is what we really need!"

And now King Colin and his men
And even, yes, the queen
Are the toughest, strongest knights-at-arms
The kingdom's ever seen.

And at the very thought of sweets
King Colin now just screams.
He never eats a single one . . .
Except for in his dreams!

So, boys and girls, remember this,
Whatever else you do,
If you can't stop eating sweets
   Just please . . .
        watch out for dragon poo!